Newark
Tales

Margaret Granger

Five Leaves Publications

Newark Tales

Margaret Granger

Published in 2001
by Five Leaves Publications,
PO Box 81,
Nottingham NG5 4ER
www.fiveleaves.co.uk

Thanks are due to Tim Warner and other staff at
Newark Library for their assistance, and to David
Ottewell for providing the cover illustration

Five Leaves acknowledge financial support
from East Midlands Arts

east **midlands**
arts
making creative
opportunities

ISBN 0 907123 98 8

Typeset by Four Sheets Design and Print
Printed by Technical Print Services, Nottingham

CONTENTS

Swift Nick

Swift Nick was the name given to Newark's best known highwayman by Charles II when he issued a proclamation offering a reward for his recapture. The real name of this man was John Nevinson (1639-1684).

Ringing for Gopher **39**

From the twelfth Sunday before Christmas each year, for six weeks, the bells of Newark Parish Church are rung for an hour. This custom began because a bequest was left by a Dutchman called Gopher in thankfulness for being safely guided to Newark by the sound of the bells. He had been lost on the Trent marshes on a foggy evening over three hundred years ago.

The Rebel Stone **43**

This is a stone marked *Here lieth a rebel, 1746,* thought to mark the burial place of a Jacobite prisoner who died while being taken to London for trial.

Fortune Telling **51**

Donald Wolfit was born at Balderton and was encouraged in amateur dramatics by Mrs Lewis Ransome, wife of the Director of Ransome and Marles. She was formerly a popular actress with the D'Oyley Carte Company. The Reverend Cyril Walker built a theatre in the vicarage grounds at Averham where Donald Wolfit acted, and afterwards became Patron.

The Monk's Tale

At nine years of age, few boys have a sense of vocation, let alone think about becoming a monk. Until I saw my father killed on his own threshold, I was scarcely awake to the world at all. Certainly I never thought of my place in it.

The manor where we lived was not large or grand, my father being only a knight in the service of the Bishop of Lincoln at his castle of Newark, but it was my whole universe. As children do, I heard people talk about the great unrest in the land since King Richard had been captured and held to ransom. I tried the words on my tongue and liked the sound, it gave me shivers of excitement. Then the men who claimed to be followers of Prince John came, demanding yet more taxes to pay the ransom. We had no money, and so they torched the thatch and killed as many as could not escape to the woods through the thick smoke.

Terror gave me more speed than the others. I covered a great distance and never saw any of my father's villeins again. I wandered for days with no knowledge of how to feed myself, seeking shelter in thickets, plastered with mud, torn by briars. I feared wild beasts, for I had never left our gatehouse before unless accompanied by my father's squire, Geoffrey, who had taught me to ride and made me practise with sword and bow.

In desperate hunger I scoured my recollection of which berries and wild foods were good to eat, but they did not satisfy and I longed for meat without the means or cunning to obtain it.

One afternoon when there was warm sun, I came to the edge of the wood where a clear stream ran into a grassy meadow, widening into a pool fringed with reeds and willow. Feeling light-headed and faint, I sat dazed and homesick by the water's edge.

When I saw the fat trout basking at my feet, I remembered how I had heard tickling described as a means of capturing them. This I could try, although my thoughts did not go as far as killing and cooking them.

It took little time to seize a fine large fish, but I had not reckoned on its slippery nature, nor on the way it would jump and wriggle for life. I missed my footing and fell face down in the shallow water, filling mouth and nose with the fine silt from the bottom.

I was jerked out of peril by my coat, and the largest hands I had ever seen were clearing my face of the choking mud with a bundle of dry grass.

"A fine fisherman you are, poaching my Lord Abbot's trout on the Sabbath," said a huge monk, "What's your name and where do you come from?"

It was many days since I had spoken to anyone, and my nights had been restless, full of dreams of smoke, flames, and blood. I tried to answer but the words would not come. The monk was looking searchingly at me. I could do nothing but sob.

"Well, that won't get us very far," he said, "here, drink this — not too much mind. I call it *aqua mirabilis*, and it contains many things to help restore you. Just a sip, now, for some of the ingredients would help you into the other world instead of bringing you back to this."

He held a tiny horn phial to my lips and I tasted a drop of exquisite sweetness, followed by a bitter after-taste. My limbs and trunk which had been chilled by the ducking felt glowing warm, then I seemed to float.

"There, nothing to worry about, is there?" said the big monk and I was on his horse in front of him, leaning against his broad chest. "I am called Brother Ambrose, from Swineshead Abbey. I will take you there now, to the infirmary until you are well."

So began my apprenticeship for whatever I now am. Because I could read and write, I was prepared for my vows, and since I no longer had a home or parents, and here at Swineshead I was fed, sheltered and protected, it seemed to me that this was the way my life was intended. At nine years old most boys accept what fate sends them.

I had no vocation, but Swineshead has gained rather than lost by my presence. I have kept my vow of obedience, even to the ultimate, as you shall see.

Whatever my faults, I have loved the abbey above all else in this world. Its beauty to eye and ear enthralled me; but above all, the minute ordering of every day, every hour, gave structure to my unformed soul.

Discipline gives freedom. There is no conflict or difficulty when one rule is accepted and adhered to. Decisions do not have to be reached, they are already made. Since it was ordained that I should enter the abbey and become a monk, that I should do to the best of my ability. I willed it, just as I willed that one day I would be as tall as Brother Ambrose, and so I was, but with more dignity and authority.

I learned all he could teach me of herbs and medicine, and with that knowledge as foundation I furthered my store of wisdom by study and experience.

King Richard returned only briefly from his imprisonment and then was away to France, fighting to regain the lands taken by King Philip, and by the time I ended my novitiate, he was dead, and also Arthur his nephew who should have been king after him. John then had no-one to gainsay him the crown until the barons rose up against him and made him sign the Great Charter. After that John defied everyone, even the Pope, and brought down an interdict upon us so that no burials, marriages, or important services of any kind could be held in full, and the common people were desolate.

The barons besieged Lincoln, and John came to relieve it. He was successful and turned south towards Dover where Prince Louis was occupying the castle, the barons having invited him over to take the English crown. On his way, John burned the farms of Crowland Abbey and there were those that said it was a judgment for this that caused him to be overtaken by the tide when crossing the Wash and so to lose all his treasure and stores.

He came, sick or despairing, to Swineshead and the Lord

3

Abbot bade me attend him since I was now infirmarian.

All that I had heard of John led me to expect a squat and ugly creature, but I saw rather the frightened and defiant youngest son of powerful parents, growing in the shadow of a popular brother, always envious and unhappy. He had the long Plantagenet frame, elegant if somewhat drooping, and a disconsolate expression.

I ordered a warm bath, with cheering essences of lavender and marigold, meanwhile I would assemble a cordial to ward off the damp chills and dispel the stomach cramps which were severe enough to bring sweat to his countenance.

My Lord Abbot came to watch me at my work.

"You have great skill, Gilbert," he said as I pounded and stirred. "What say you of his Majesty's health?"

"Maybe he is distressed at his great loss and exhausted from the journey, Father."

"No doubt. You have heard of the farms that have been destroyed at Crowland?"

"It will be hard for the peasants with winter approaching and their crops gone," I answered.

"And for the brothers and those who depend on their hospitality. You remember, Gilbert, that some five years back our brothers at Louth Park were robbed of 1,680 marks?"

Much had been said of John taking money from the Church; it seemed a greater sin than taking lives and livelihoods.

"What are you making?" he asked, sniffing at the potion I had almost finished.

"A little restorative for his Majesty's stomach," I said.

"Is it not the King's heart that is at fault?"

"Perhaps, but that will heal better if his bodily ills are cured," I said.

"We are the instruments of God, Gilbert," said my Lord Abbot taking his leave. "His Majesty intends to go to Sleaford; I hope he will be well enough to travel."

My hope was that he would be able to journey beyond monastic houses. From one cause or another, the King was

4

likely to die. With both barons and people in a state of revolt, the Church would make a ready scapegoat.

I took the potion to the King. Bathed and dressed in a richly coloured robe, he already looked better. His eyes, bright and alert, searched my face, and I was careful to keep my features composed.

"I feel much revived after your excellent bath," he said. "What is your name, brother?"

I told him, and noticed a small flickering muscle at the corner of his mouth.

"I have here an elixir that will ease you still more, if it please you, Sire," I said.

His eyes even keener, he kept them on my face while he beckoned to a boy nearby who came forward, poured a little of my *aqua mirabilis* into a cup and swallowed it.

"Leave the rest there," John said, "in an hour, if all is well, I will take it."

I bowed and left, being well-suited with the arrangement.

By next day I had prepared more and awaited a summons to his room.

"Brother Gilbert," he said, "I have had such a sleep this night as I have not known since childhood, and I awakened like a child, without heaviness."

"That is because it is not a sleeping draught, your Majesty," I said, "My *aqua mirabilis* contains no valerian, mandragora or poppy. If you take more now, you will not be drowsy, but simply strengthened. You slept only because your body was eased and weariness could be naturally relieved."

"It is well-named," he said, "Is it your own invention?"

"Not entirely," I said, "Brother Ambrose who was infirmarian before me gave me the basic formula. Finding it somewhat bitter, I changed the constituents a little to make it more palatable. I find honey beneficial for many ills, and its inclusion also sweetens."

Father Abbot himself came to tell me I was to accompany the king to Sleaford, with such remedies as were

5

required for the King's journey to Dover.

"Stay as long as his Majesty desires, Gilbert," he said, "but leave instruction for Brother Nicholas who will take your place."

As I expected, the King was strengthened for the journey, but began again to suffer at Sleaford Castle where I had thought to leave him. Feeling perhaps his extremity, he decided to press on to Newark and there I must go too.

Accordingly, I adjusted the dose so that for two days he was able to attend to matters of state, writing much, including his will. Then, his torment increasing, he confessed and received the sacrament.

The terrible seventeen years of his reign were over and England could hope again. As for me, I was happy to return to Swineshead, which was the reason for my existence. As I rode nearer to that beloved place, I thought of the Prince who would now be King. His age was nine years.

Saint Catherine's Well

A castle is not the place to bring up a daughter. Even in peace, there is too soldierly an atmosphere, too little gentleness and grace. Yet my Isabel was like her name, fair and pleasing, a contrast to the grey prison by the River Trent that was Newark Castle.

It was a busy time for me as Custodian of the castle. Edward, third king of that name, was warring with the Scots and this proved expensive and troublesome in two ways. Firstly, when the Scots came to treat with him for a settlement, Newark was asked to accommodate some thirty persons and provide such comfort as courtesy required. Both my time and substance were taken up with this, but more than that, the town was taxed heavily to pay for supplies for the King's army, much to the chagrin of the populace, which made my position uneasy.

Isabel, her mother having died while she was yet a child, therefore spent much of her time in the company of her maids, which I had chosen for their years and sobriety. In this I may have been wrong, thinking a staid example to be best. It may be that she found their discourse tedious, and there being no younger women to divert her, she began to notice the many young men who were constantly visiting and staying within the castle walls.

I saw no harm in Sir Everard Bevercotes who was our near neighbour, being Lord of the Manor at Balderton. It pleased me to know that my only child would not be too far removed on the occasion of her marriage. Having no sons, I was anxious for grandchildren, being now possessed of property within the town and hoping to bestow it early upon my heirs. Therefore I was well pleased when Isabel looked for the coming of Sir Everard each day, and it was clear that she preferred him to his friend, Sir Guy Saucemere, who also appeared to think himself a favourite.

As I said, there was much to keep me occupied at that time, and I must confess I thought my daughter happily entertained with her two suitors, too young to take either seriously. Isabel had great beauty, of that calm and placid mould which a father may accept as innocence. Maybe she was innocent; I believe it in truth, but unhappily she grew so fond of Sir Everard that she walked and talked with him alone, and Sir Guy heard of this. Given the situation in the castle at the time, some of the many who were there would readily observe them and note their growing affection. Fighting men gossip almost as much as old dames at the parish pump. They have time on their hands and nothing else to fill it, so Sir Guy learned of his friend's deceit.

They told me afterwards that he took it sullenly, probably in vanity fancying himself the favourite. He was the least well-looking and I have often observed such young men to be the most vain of their appeal to women.

But my lovely Isabel was all unaware of his discovery, as was Sir Everard, who came visiting as usual in the dusk of the last day of April, St. Catherine's. Sir Everard returned by moonlight following the path by the Devon water. There Guy lay in wait with his drawn sword.

He attacked with great suddenness and ferocity, almost severing Everard's head from his body. It is said that in the place where Everard fell, a spring of clear water arose, but that was not disclosed at the time, and Guy, being afraid lest he be discovered there and meet with due punishment, took the ancient Roman road we call the Fosse Way to Nottingham.

There he met with a party of pilgrims going to Rome and joined them. He remained abroad for many years, and since his disappearance was noticed to be at the same time as his former friend's death, tongues soon began to put the two events together.

Isabel began to peak and grow frail, taking no pleasure in her garden within the curtain wall, nor in her pet birds, her music or her needlework. Other suitors would gladly have taken the place of those who were gone, but she moped and dwindled to her grave, while I grew old and bitter. One evening I was returning late to the castle when I saw and smelt a shambling figure in the buttress corner of the gatehouse wall. By the hoarse voice that replied to my challenge, I knew him for a leper and moved to the far side of the gate, fearing contagion. Yet I threw him a coin, mindful of my Christian duty.

"Alan Cauldwell," he said, "what of your daughter Isabel?"

"Isabel died," I said, "who asks?"

He made a sound, half sigh, half groan, full of weariness and sickness, so that I thought he might die here in the gateway before morning as vagrants sometimes did. It concerned me that the infection might come among the garrison where it would spread disastrously, but he seemed to read my mind and moved further off, ape-like and shuffling with the tell-tale stiffness of the disease.

"I loved sweet Isabel," he said, and vanished into the night.

Before long, the town which had been oppressed with such heavy taxation, including half the wool brought to its warehouses, all at once became a place of more interest and hope. Throughout the taverns, gossip buzzed of a miraculous healing well, hard by the Devon water.

A leper, they said, had been cured there, and become the guardian of the place.

Rumour grew that the well was fed by a spring which appeared when Sir Everard was stabbed, and the guardian was none other than Sir Guy, repentant and devout. While he was overseas, suffering and diseased, St. Catherine herself had appeared to him in a dream and told him to seek healing at the scene of his crime.

It is a story for minstrels and word-spinners; I am too old to believe easily in the magical and sudden appearance of a spring in a watery place, although he who once was Sir Guy Saucemere may well be known now as Guthred, thought by some to be a saint. As for the healing, I have long known that those with faith may find it in water, or

9

in the laying on of hands, or in almost any outward sign which satisfies the mind, for that is what priests tell us is the work of Christ.

My days draw to their close in loneliness. Now that I have given over my duties to others there is time to think and remember, and also to read. One Geoffrey Chaucer, who has also been a soldier, writes much to my liking and helps me to people my shadow world with those who used to inhabit it. Instead of regret, he gives me comfort when I ponder such words as these:

> *For all that cometh, cometh of necessity;*
> *Thus to be lorn, it is my destiny.*

Long after I am gone, it may be that the people of Newark will read this curious history and wonder at its sad strangeness. Yet I dare say their own times will produce tales equally unfathomable.

The Master Surgeon

It is not given to many daughters to govern a father's household as I did. The people of Newark marvelled to see how from the age of four, when my mother died leaving me her only child, father took me with him to the wool warehouses daily. He began to teach me to tally the packs, watch them being sealed and see the ponies trotting out from The White Hart to take the road to Lincoln where the stable is.

Naturally, living in such a prominent position, I was noticed by all who came to the town, and soon became aware of the attention. In consequence I regarded myself queen of every gathering, although I must say I worked hard for this recognition.

Some time after noon on a damp and raw day in early spring I heard the flurry of arrival and looked down from a casement over the entrance. A small man was having some difficulty dismounting, no doubt having ridden a considerable distance. He had a string of two or three pack horses and was accompanied by a manservant.

"Good day to you Sir," I said having hastened to meet him, "How can we oblige you? A private chamber, with a fire and some refreshment?"

He straightened and I felt his keen gaze go through me like a knife. With so many workmen and boys about as well as the careless maids, Annis, my good aunt who lived with us, always ensured I was neatly coifed and fittingly gowned. I made a composed courtesy, slow enough to show that I was no underling.

Nodding briefly, he said, "Hot water will suffice, in a pot to go on the fire. I am John Arderne, lately come from London."

I caught my breath, knowing the plague was raging there, but he said, calmly, "Do not fear. It is true I have been among the pestilence because I can sometimes work

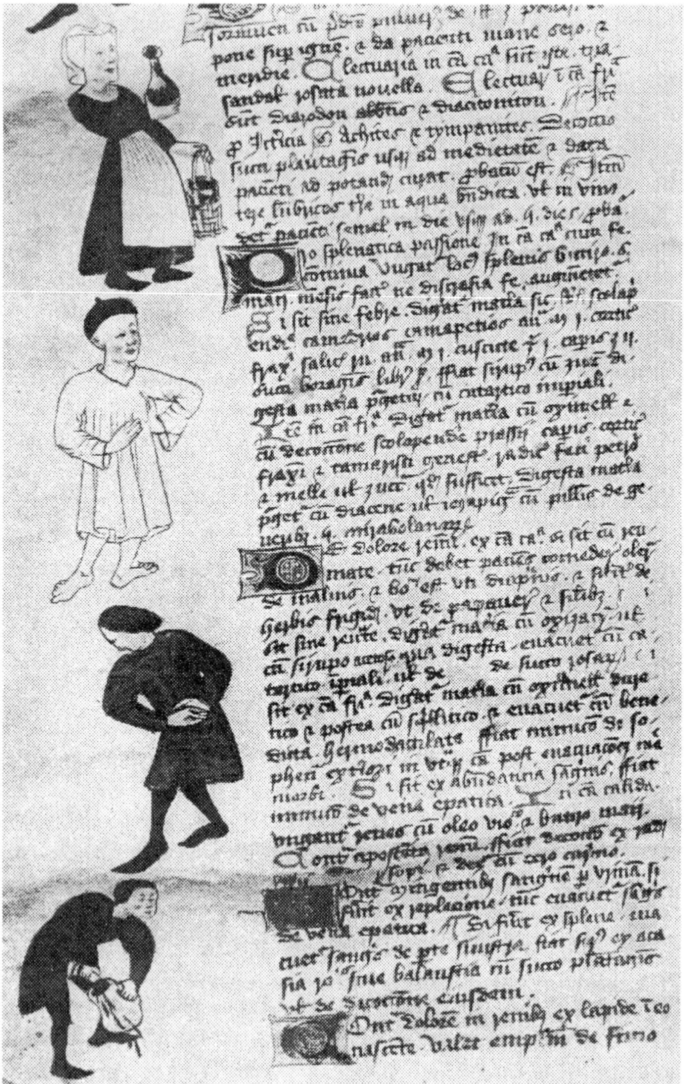

cures, but I would not risk my own life, and I will not endanger others."

He then gave instructions to his serving man who took one bag into the inn, leaving the rest for the varlets.

I went to see to the bringing of the water, and when I brought a scullion with a skillet, the serving man added a few dried herbs and said, "Let it be heated a little more."

While he attended to the decoction, I saw that the herbs had come from a most beautiful box of black wood, chased with silver in a curious design. Inside it was divided into compartments, each with its own separate wooden lid, except for one which contained a small vessel with a silver cap. From this the serving man had taken powder, using for the purpose a tiny spoon which also had its own secure place within the box.

The smell from the skillet was heady and spicy. "A restorative for tired travellers," said the visitor, "and possibly a preventative against disease."

"Is he a doctor then?" asked my father when I told him.

"More of a scholar, I believe," I said, "for I noticed he carried a great many manuscripts."

"Hmmm," said my father, his countenance closed and wary, "I want no necromancy here." He had misliked the description of the box which so fascinated me.

Next day when they met, my father greeted him civilly as "Master" and entered into conversation concerning the progress of the plague. My father was ever cautious at admitting travellers from places known to be affected.

"The pestilence breeds in poverty, as I am sure you know," said Master Arderne, "for the most part because of lack of cleanliness. Where houses are ill-kept and vermin breed, where clothes and bodies lack regular washing, and where food is handled carelessly, all for lack of time and sufficient pence, there you will find the contagion."

My father was nodding sagely at this, being a member of the Guild of the Holy Trinity which did much to help the poor. They said that this was for the health of the whole populace as well as to the glory of God.

All talk of sorcery was forgotten and Master Arderne considered a man of sound sense. This pleased me, for I was curious as to the nature of the manuscripts, though I knew they would be in Latin of which I had only a little.

"I should think not indeed, Winifrede," scolded Annis, "Do you want to be taken for a witch? Ill enough that you can read and account as well as any man, let alone the Latin."

"Holy nuns know Latin," I replied, but seeing her reproving look said, "Your pardon, good Aunt."

My father smiled a little, but straightened his features as he caught her glance. "Get about your work, Daughter," he said.

As I left, Annis said to him, "It is time you remembered that she is your daughter, not your son. She is thirteen, would you not wish her well married?"

"Not while I find her such good help. Time enough for marrying when she wishes it. Winifrede has sense enough to choose a husband of ability, and meanwhile, the more she learns, the better she will manage her own affairs."

Pondering this I went to a little garth where I had planted some herbs. It was sheltered, and although still early in the year, I hoped that some of them would be putting forth shoots. Winter salt meat needs considerable flavouring.

"Winifrede child, does your garden contain sweet chervil?" I heard Master Arderne say, and turned to see him at the entrance.

"I do not know chervil, Sir," I said.

"An excellent salad," he said, "but it should be sown early. I see you have a good variety of herbs, do you know their properties?"

"Some," I said, "but I would like to know more than just their use in cooking."

"That is well," he answered. "The chervil I just spoke of is a wonderful protection against infection. You should cultivate it lest the plague begins to reach here."

The following day, Master Arderne went out to mingle

14

with those attending the market for he had a great curiosity and a good ear for the gossip of all sorts and conditions of people.

"Winifrede," he said when he came in, "Do you know this Adam de Everingham?"

"I think he is like to die," I answered.

"I fear that is true," said Annis, "Winifrede, your father has returned and he will want you with parchment and pen directly."

Annis sent me away fearing that Master Arderne would speak of the fistula which it was believed would kill Adam Everingham. Long hours in the saddle in full armour made this a common complaint among soldiers, and Sir Adam had consulted physicians and surgeons in France, suffering a number of operations. He had now returned to his manor of Laxton, and few thought he would ever leave it again.

"Laxton is somewhat remote, and known as Laxton in the Clay for the heavy nature of its soil," I told Master Arderne. "It lies to the north west, close by Tuxford, but you will find the road impassable after rain, the clay is clinging as birdlime."

He laughed. "Tell me, child," he said, "Have you these by you?" He passed me a manuscript roll.

"The necessary ingredients for this compound, Sir? Well, they are few enough, but I do not have Honey of Roses."

"Do you know where it can be obtained?"

"There is a woman lives outside the town in the Northgate, Rosa by name, who sometime brings such things into the market. Or I could go to her," I said.

"Rosa is a known witch, you must not go," said Annis.

"Winifrede shall direct me, I will go myself," said Master Arderne. Annis became big-eyed and fearful as I told him the way to Rosa's hovel which was on the way to Lincoln, I had passed it often with my father.

Living close by the market, with all kinds of persons attending, I had no delicate fancies concerning the ills of

the body, but already, at the age of thirteen, I loved that
which was healthy and beautiful. Therefore the work of
Master Arderne held great interest for me. All ills had
somewhere a cure in nature and I had a strong desire to
know those remedies.

I knew the nature of fistula, and that Master Arderne's
treatment involved cutting and removing the pile, and
afterwards cleansing thoroughly. Clearly the compound
was to heal the cut after the fistula had been removed,
being a soothing mixture containing eggs. It seemed good
to me, providing the eggs were fresh and from fowl which
were cleanly kept.

"Ah," said Master Arderne, "You believe that important?"

"Certainly, Sir," I said, "for the egg is a living thing
which can breed infection. Placed on a wound, such infection would mortify."

"As you have said, many times Sir," said Gregory his
manservant, and I was abashed at the clear approval of
both men, though I saw they were a little amused also.

Master Arderne and Gregory were gone for a sennight
or more, and made returns to Laxton over some six
months, but were always cheerful. At last they told that
Adam de Everingham had ridden on horseback without
difficulty and shown his gratitude with a purse of one hundred shillings and much praise, which brought many
important sufferers to seek out the great surgeon.

Master Arderne now required a house where he could
practise his skills freely and receive those from all parts
who sought him out. It was a sad day when he departed
from The White Hart, but the instruction I had from him
became Annis's chief topic of conversation, endowing me
with wisdom and knowledge far beyond my modest ability.

Since I had shown an interest in healing, some came for
relief from their afflictions, knowing well that I would not
attempt what was unseemly to my nature, and abiding
always by the rules of the Physician.

Master Arderne remained in the town for a score of

years, becoming famous throughout England, journeying forth to restore health to the great and wealthy. He wrote his first book while in Newark, and numerous manuscripts beside. On his return to London, he wrote more and became a Master Surgeon.

Despite this, he maintained that his cures were due to Providence, saying of any proposed treatment, "Nevertheless, do another man as him thinketh best."

Which seems to me the wisest way for any healer.

Minster Lovell

Lord Lovell at Stoke Field, 1487

There was peace in Minster Lovell. The honey colour of stone cottages gave a glow of prosperity, the river wound gently round the old manor house, a swan reflected in the tree-fringed waters. A man who left this place for any cause would feel an ache in his heart ever afterwards.

I felt sure Frances Lovell had returned here.

How had he fared since crossing the Trent that night after the battle? Better than I, no doubt, who foolish, penniless and lame, still came seeking a defeated rebel who had supported the House of York against Lancaster. A wealthy Lord, though now, whether he had been drowned or slain on the battlefield as some thought, his many estates would be taken.

But I knew that he lived, or at least that neither of the other presumptions was true.

It had been a long journey from Stoke-by-Newark, dangerous at times. Henry Tudor's men, driven by that tight-lipped man, grimly hunted down any that were of an age to have fought for the Earl of Warwick, or as some would have it, the imposter Lambert Simnel, who had been crowned King Edward VI in Ireland.

I was no rebel, nor indeed able to bear arms, but the country had been unsettled by strife for many generations, and since Richard had died at Bosworth, Henry of Lancaster's men grew ever more ruthless. Even a crippled wanderer such as I would be suspect, either as spy or wounded deserter. I had been born with a twisted back and a limp, but soldiers would not trouble to enquire how my infirmities had been caused.

Truth to tell, I had never been of much account until I met Frances, Viscount Lovell. Stoke is a humble village, dependent for survival on some few acres of ground between the marshland by the River Trent and the old Roman road called the Fosse Way. I was a by-blow, some said with a noble father, and therefore I was given the name of Markham after a much despised Lord of the Manor of nearby Cotham. Certainly I was given advantages that my mother could not have afforded from her earnings, which were casual, although she had skills.

I was taught to read and write, and more, an old monk gave me instruction in herbs and medicines, a subject which captured my interest. I spent many hours searching for rare herbs and studying their properties in books, which were my greatest treasure. It was in this capacity that I met Lord Lovell, for he came himself to ask for my help in doctoring a friend of his who had suffered grievously from deep and dangerous cuts caused by the edge of a heavy sword.

Among many things I had not understood about warfare was that in such close hand-to-hand fighting, swords were not used with a quick clean thrust, for they were too difficult to withdraw. More damage was effected by slashing furiously at the enemy, thus disabling many in the time it would take to kill one. It was tiring work, and two hours into the battle, many men were wearied, scarcely knowing friend from enemy.

We at Stoke had never expected the battle to be on our demesne. Newark was the important place, with castle and town defences. We had nothing but our fields and the river flowing between us and Fiskerton. But the rebels had forded the river there, and King Henry's men had come from Radcliffe-on-Trent, pinching our poor village between them.

Knowing only what I had read, which was mostly of the glory and honour of war, I crept towards our little church and secreted myself among the yew trees there. I could see the clean grooves by the door where waiting soldiers had sharpened their swords. Such knowledge made me feel old, almost a man.

When the sounds of fighting came I was amazed that the human voice rang loud over the hiss of arrows, clash of steel, awesome explosions from the cannon and sharp reports of the hand-guns newly arrived from Germany. I heard the screams of men for the first time; and worse, the screams of horses.

At that time, the rebel forces had not lost the ascendent and Francis was moving about freely, encouraging the men, smiling cheerily at his friends. So it was that, finding one wounded, and hearing from a soldier that I was near and had some remedies with me, he sought me out.

It was just at the turn of the battle. Francis did not yet know, but Martin Schwartz, captain of the professional soldiers, had been killed and the Yorkists began to lose heart. I was aware someone of importance had died but found it difficult to work out what cause either side was fighting for. It would make no difference to the cottagers of Stoke; they would still work for little or nothing whether Henry of Lancaster or Edward of York was on the throne.

There were camp followers in plenty waiting at a safe distance to care for the wounded, and I could do little more than offer a draught of water to those unable to reach help. It seemed to me I would have been wiser to stay within doors, knowing nothing of such unimaginable horror. I closed my eyes, but still saw raw open wounds gaping like protesting mouths.

I felt a strong hand on my shoulder and a voice asked, "Are you the boy apothecary who carries specifics to ease pain?"

"I have a few," I said, "not enough for the needs of all, therefore I dare not use them here."

"There is one in great need, a man dear to me. Come, for he lies some distance apart."

I was sad indeed when we arrived, for it was too late. The man was one I had seen earlier who seemed certain of victory for the Yorkists. His name was Michael de la Pole, Earl of Lincoln, and I had noted his confident gallantry, though they said he had first been Henry's supporter and later moved over to the Yorkists. Now he lay dead of a gun wound in the breast.

Lord Lovell had turned away, cast down but refusing to let it be seen. He spoke earnestly and quietly to another, and I surmised they concluded the day was lost.

The other departed, and Lord Lovell stood looking where there was a steep ravine full of desperately wounded men beset by Henry's troops on either bank. Even so, some emerged through the exit onto the marshes, still pursued and harried, making for the river bank where they had landed only three hours ago.

"No use that way," said Lord Lovell to himself, then to me, "Markham, I need a place to shelter, at least until darkness, perhaps longer."

He must have seen how shocked I was that he whom I had thought a leader, nobly caring for a wounded friend, should prove a skulking coward when he saw his comrades butchered in retreat.

"Of what use would I be to the young king, dead?" he asked. "Somehow I must get safe away from here. Can you help?"

Perhaps I could. I would if it meant that the poor ten-year-old they had brought to this carnage was given his life.

There was a place close by the church which I had discovered when searching for hemlock, which because of its poisonous nature is not tolerated near any dwelling, although used outwardly it is without peer. Some night-watcher had leaned timber against an ancient wall to shelter him, and over all the brambles had grown. The entrance to this concealment was small and low. Within, there was room for a man to lie at full-length.

We walked as if to reach the higher ground where men held conference, unsure as yet of who could claim victory, for the losses had been as great on both sides. Only when deaths among the leaders were known would the outcome be sure.

Once screened from his enemies by the trees, I told Lord Lovell how to find the hiding place, and urging him to keep out of sight as far as possible, make his way there through the woods.

I went alone back to the village. Doors were still closed, windows shuttered this bright June afternoon. Relieved at the absence of the smell compounded of blood, ordure, smoke and sweat, I crept thankfully into my cottage.

At twilight people began to emerge from their homes. I put a little food in a cloth and went with a small group who felt the need to pray in the church, talking with them of what I had seen earlier.

"And you say Henry Tudor has won the day, Markham? What has befallen the boy they said was crowned in Ireland, the new King Edward?"

"I did not see him," I said, and saw their disappointment. A boy of ten who had escaped imprisonment and been made king of the rebels drew their hearts. Henry was known as a stern man; they would have liked a king they could love.

"I hear he has been captured, over by Southwell," said one.

"Poor little mite," said a woman, "he'll need our prayers."

It was easy to slip away from the church door in the gathering darkness. By the secret entrance to the hide I whispered, "My Lord?"

"Come," he said, drawing himself up into little compass, and I sat on the earth beside him.

He drank thirstily, and ate a little food, then picked up a small phial I had put in the cloth. "What is this?" he asked.

"Forgive me, my Lord," I said, "I thought if you were captured you might wish to make your own quietus. It is hemlock — also useful for external inflammations."

"I thank you, Markham," he said and stowed it carefully within his doublet.

"They have driven willow stakes through the hearts of my Lord Lincoln and Captain Schwartz," I said, and saw him wince, "and the little king is taken prisoner."

"It is time to go," he said.

"Where?" I asked.

23

"To my home in Oxfordshire, Minster Lovell," he said.

I led him, under cover of the chancy summer dark, slowly down towards the river. The Trent is unlovely here, flowing sullenly through dank marshes, but it is neither wide nor deep in summer. He gained the opposite shore and disappeared.

King Henry had vouchsafed to clear the land of corpses and debris, but that night there were many horrors encountered on my lonely return. My thoughts were with the man I had known so briefly, and when I reached my house I found I could not rest.

Dawn found me walking along the High Fosse the way Henry's troops had marched two days before. It was safe enough, they were carousing in Newark Castle. After reaching Radcliffe I pressed on towards Leicester, still keeping to the old Roman road which during many days took me most of the way to Minster Lovell. The Manor House had been in the possession of the Crown ever since Lord Lovell had fought at Bosworth, and fled from there to Flanders. I knew by the nervous manner of the villagers that I was not the only stranger to appear after the battle at Stoke. Henry's men were watching against his return.

I knew that my presence would endanger Lord Lovell and departed circumspectly, certain that he had reached home.

In 1708 during alterations to the Manor House at Minster Lovell, the skeleton of a man was discovered in an underground room, seated at a table with books, papers and pen before him. The assumption was that because for some reason a trusted servant had been unable to come to him, he had starved to death. The position in which he was found made this seem unlikely. Hemlock was commonly used for external injuries, but Culpeper warns of its poisonous nature.

24

The Carter's Tale

They call me John Carter, but that's not my real name. John Carter died a few months back of the hot sickness some said was the plague. Truth to tell, I don't rightly remember my name, for it's a long time since I left Leicestershire where I was born. Now and again I think of the home I used to have, and my mother bustling round the fire, but that's mostly when I see another woman at her work. It seems I slip out of one kitchen into another, but my eyes go queer on me and I can't be sure whether I'm seeing or dreaming.

One thing I can remember is my father going off to fight, and that was over twenty years ago. My mother wept and stormed, then said she would follow him, for how could she stay and hold up her head in our village when he was lifting his hand against the king?

My father was much angered that my mother would not stay safe at home, and he was right, for when the king surrendered at Newark, she was already dying from the privations suffered traipsing after the New Model Army. We had seen nothing of my father since the successful engagement at Naseby, and so at five years old I was orphaned among people whose sympathies were mostly with the defeated Royalists.

Fortunately I was too young to be frightened at my situation. Being an only child, I was used to much petting on account of my curls and sweet smile which always called forth comment. Moreover, during these last months I had learned to accept discomfort with some philosophy, and to appreciate kindness with winning gratitude.

Therefore when John Carter called at The Olde White Hart where I was lodging with some stable lads, he was amused to see me strutting out to help with his horse, although it was as much as I could do to lift an empty bucket, let alone a full one.

25

Holme Church showing Nan Scott's Chamber

"What's your name?" he asked, and "Ironside!" they shouted to tease me.

I did not mind, for I knew the Ironsides had won and perhaps Oliver Cromwell would be made king. If he was, I would go to London and find my father, and we could go back to Leicestershire.

Whenever John Carter came after for the Wednesday market, he called for his Little Ironside, and took me into the inn to share his meal. Then one day he asked me if I would like to go to his village, called Holme, to look after his pigs, sheep and chickens.

"You would be company for Nan," he said, "when I'm away."

"Who's Nan?" I asked, not really interested.

"Nan Scott's my grand-daughter," he said, "she's older than you, but the farm work's heavy for her. Besides, there's strangers roaming the countryside after all the fighting. You're not very big, but you're a bright lad and could look out for her a bit. Leastways, she wouldn't be on her own."

A girl. I could not remember girls, except the shameless hoydens who followed the soldiers and had been whipped and worse by the commanders. The stable lads were rough at times, but I managed to keep out of their way when they'd had too much ale, which wasn't often. Truth to tell, there was very little of ale or anything else in those days, especially work for money. The siege had been long, the people were shabby and many were hungry.

Men were busy pulling down the castle, many of the shops had been burned, and there were warnings about the plague again. Controls were being put into operation concerning hucksters coming to market in case they brought the infection. Sometimes I wondered if I would be driven away, like the stray cats and dogs. When I heard a man had been appointed to knock them on the head, I had bad dreams and screamed aloud. The lads laughed, or sometimes swore and cuffed me.

I felt the eyes of the innkeeper, potboys and scullery

27

maids all on me, and sensed they wanted me gone. An extra mouth to feed, nobody's child and getting in the way more often than not, I might as well go to this Holme that John Carter talked about. When the good times came back to Newark, so would I.

It was a low-lying village, and from the first I hated the way the mist hung over the River Trent in the early hours of the morning. The grazing cattle seemed to have no legs, and they, like the sheep, coughed fearsomely. But I found Nan Scott to be a cheerful girl, a good cook, with plenty of common sense.

The parson, not having a house there, had a little room over the church porch where he taught the boys to read and cast figures. When he found me quick to learn, he gave me little tasks about the church which I performed gladly. Like Nan, I preferred to be there rather than in the house, which was dark and small. Holme church was by no means big, but there was light enough and space to move.

John Carter brought the wine for the Holy Communion from Newark, and it was stored in that little south-facing room over the porch. It was always two flagons of the best, for as John said, Parson needed something that would keep out the chill of the river mist when he had to walk back across the fields by night.

At first I did the work around the little farmyard, and helped John with his horse when he came back from market, but as I grew, he began to take me into town with him on Wednesdays to help lift the loads.

It was good to see Newark prosper again, and there were those at the White Hart who remembered me as a starveling child. Now I was grown a strong lad. By and by I began to dream of one day being carter in John's stead.

But just as trade seemed to be picking up and stores were filled with goods for sale, some ten years after one king was beheaded and we had another on the throne in place of the Lord Protector, the plague returned.

One evening when John set out with me to go home, he did not take the reins, but sat beside me hunched and silent as we picked our way through the river mist.

"Take the wine to the church," he said when we reached the farmyard, "then see to the horse."

When I returned to the cart, he was not there, but Nan came bustling out with a full basket.

"Grandfather says I am to take this to the porch chamber, then fetch bedclothes," she said. "What's amiss, John?"

"I think he may have the infection," I said. "Where is he?"

"Somewhere about the yard," she said, "but he will not come in the house."

I found him later putting a red cross on the door. "Fetch what you need," he said, "then go and find a lodging for yourself in the buildings. Nan is to sleep in the porch chamber until the plague clears, but do not you go near either her or the neighbours."

He need have given no such warning. For three days as I tended the horse and the rest of the animals, no-one approached me. On the third day, I saw the parson leave the house with a white cover over the Communion cup. That afternoon I followed John Carter's body to the church yard, and saw Nan's face at the window of the porch chamber.

There were two other burials that day. More and more followed, until Parson no longer said the service separately but over as many as ten souls at once. At least here it was not as in Newark where they purchased a special piece of land and put all in a common grave.

At each funeral I looked for Nan's face. It grew paler and thinner, and I feared her food would not last, and hoped she was making use of the Communion wine. I resolved to take her some milk from the many cows I milked each day, their owners being dead; for I argued that freshly drawn it would not carry the infection.

Having indicated by way of the window that I would leave the milk at the foot of the little turret stair for her, I went away, and for the first time in many weeks walked along the village street. There was one very fine house, but the family had either died or left. The door stood wide open, left so by looters pilfering and despoiling. Mostly they had taken drink, and having swigged it left pots and bottles all about.

So I passed dwelling after dwelling, until I came to the last and realised I had not seen a living soul.

"John," came a voice from behind me and I turned in a sudden cold sweat, feeling the hair rise in the nape of my neck.

But it was Nan, thin and weak, supporting herself with a broom handle.

"We are the last, John," she said. "All these weeks I have kept tally in the back of one of Parson's books. None else are left."

"What shall we do?" I asked.

"I think the plague must be finished now at Newark," she said. "In a day or two you can go and see. Take them milk, and when I am stronger I will make butter and cheese. There are eggs too. Take whatever you can to relieve their need."

I did as she told me, and for a time we continued a dreamlike existence so unreal that it is no longer possible to recollect the detail. I only know we worked all the daylight hours, and I journeyed to Newark as before, then almost insensible with weariness went to my bed.

Nan remained in the porch loft, and as people began to come back to Holme, tales grew that the face at the window was no living woman but a ghost.

She might well have been. Time passed and she ceased to come to the yard. I grew to dread the work there and found myself lodgings in Newark.

Although I still made my weekly journey to Holme, I never heard that anyone had spoken with her, or entered the room which now they call Nan Scott's chamber.

After all these months they still whisper of her face appearing there and cross themselves.

It seems we shall never know what became of Nan, only

that she was the last belonging to Holme to survive the plague.

The king who was beheaded at Westminster, The Lord Protector and all the generals, will have their place in history. But who will remember a village girl who took refuge in a church and watched the funerals of all her neighbours?

They call me John Carter, but that is not my name...

Swift Nick

"Dossie!"

Confound the man, why could he never give me my name? Even when it was not this favourite that sounded to me so much like "doxey", he called me "Doll" or "Fan" or ironically "Sweetheart."

I thought at first he did it to show his dislike of a woman in his world, but young Meg and Tabby were never miscalled in any way, although they brought in half the pelf I did. Whatever I took, he showed no pleasure, but then I rode out like him; they only dabbed round the town. Newark was not bad for such pickings in the market, though not like the Great North Road. Where they might get a locket from a farmer's wife, I could take a bag of guineas or a fine necklace. I was as profitable as any of the men, but saw no credit for it. Nick smiled that year as we totalled up our grand haul of £2,000; smiled and looked all round at every one of us as we drank our triumph in The Talbot in Newark market place, but as his eyes fell on me, his smile died.

"Dossie!"

"My name is Elizabeth Burton," I said.

"Of course it is, Sweetheart," he said, "and you're just the girl, I'm thinking, to ride to Tuxford or Weston to find out what moves along the North Road come next week."

"You know the mails better than the coachmen," I said.

"Not the mails, wench, the gentry. Put on your petticoats and see if there's a silly girl blabbing about how my Lord This and Lady That will be off to court next Tuesday, with all their money and jewellery. Better still, go nuzzle up to some footman at the Blue Bell and see what he can tell you that might be profitable."

He stared hard as he spoke, at the men's clothes I wore. Suddenly I was aware of their filthy, ragged state, and petticoats were a pleasing thought, but I had no decent gowns here in Newark.

There was a woman who brought to the market gowns obtained from some of the tradesmen's wives. The ladies of Newark were purse-proud and if parting with a garment that had plenty of wear left, liked to get a few coppers in exchange. Their maids had poor pickings from the mistresses' cast-offs.

I nodded to Meg who was wearing a kirtle like a tavern wench, which many in the town took her to be, seeing her often at The Talbot. "I need skirts," I said, "but can scarcely go to buy any dressed like this. Hang on my arm and pretend I'm your swain, then coax me to buy something for you."

She thought this good sport and we set off into the market together. Meg's eye fell at once upon a gown with a wired ruff of white lace, much out of date, belonging to the time of the King's father in the days before the Commonwealth. Besides wanting something of plainer sort, I saw at once that it would be more of Meg's size, too narrow and short in the body for me.

"Won't you get me that one?" she pleaded, falling in with her part, and the woman at the stall was all attention, pointing out the quality of the material, holding it against Meg to show how it became her.

"It is useless for the purpose," I said, irritated and forgetting to keep my voice pitched low. I noticed the woman's keen glance at my face, so keeping up the charade I dragged Meg away and sent her back to the inn alone.

The market woman began to put away her smaller merchandise, muffs and collars that were displayed close, away from thieving hands. Then she spread out on the pavement a canvas roll such as pedlars carry, and became engrossed in carefully stowing the rejected garment into it. In a moment I sped across the open space to snatch another serviceable garment in dark green that hung from a pole behind her.

Bundling it into a roll, I stepped round the pole, concealed from her by some cloaks, and slipping the gown

34

under my coat, made off towards the church, thinking to return to The Talbot another way. Unfortunately, as I slipped into the alley between some houses that flanked the church, I walked into the town watchman who was beginning his evening round. My head was turned away from him, for I was looking back to see if any had noticed my theft.

His hand shot out and grasped my arm, his suspicion being aroused by my furtive attitude, and then my woman's nature gave me away. Where a man or a boy would either have stood firm and faced him out or pulled free, I shrank away at his touch.

"What's this?" he asked, and looked hard at my face, then snatched at the bulge beneath my coat. As he shook out the dress I felt myself begin to tremble, for there was still much Puritan notion in towns like Newark, and wearing man's apparel would be thought more sinful than stealing.

In the middle of the market place was a lock-up. We reached it by going past the woman from whom I had stolen the dress, and she had a great deal to say about my imposture, and my earlier attempt, with a young woman accomplice, to steal a more valuable garment. It was useless to deny, she was too voluble and inventive, so I entered the dark place where I spent a cold and hungry night.

Next morning I was taken to a nearby house, given bread and a cup of water and shown into a room where a man sat behind a table, and a clerk with ink and paper beside him.

After I had given my name I was asked questions that gave me the opportunity to lay the blame on Swift Nick, or John Nevinson, as he was properly known. The other name had been given to him by no less a person than the King, and there were some in Newark who saw a kind of glory in having a highwayman who had been recognised by Royalty staying openly at The Talbot.

I had removed my hat and let my hair fall. Humbly and

timidly, I told of the task I had been assigned, without the means to accomplish it. The listening men narrowed their eyes, pursed their lips, beginning to calculate what advantage there may be in treating this unfortunate woman leniently.

"Tell us how this — er — ring is controlled. Obviously information is brought to Nevinson by various less well-known persons such as yourself who can obtain it surreptitiously, but how does he maintain authority over this lawless gang?"

"He rides about like a great hero," I said, "and he has a companion, Edmund Bracy of Nottingham who hires a room by the year at The Talbot for the use of all Nick's acquaintances. It is very sure, for the landlord frequently whispers with Nick and Bracy. I have also seen the ostler have money from both of them, for I think he tells of those who have traded profitably in the market and are worth to be waylaid going home."

"How much is he like to get by this means?" he asked.

"There was a gentleman from London who sold silver at the markets. He was stopped between Gainsborough and Newark and relieved of £200."

"What was your share of this, Elizabeth Burton?"

"£2, may it please you Sir," I said.

"And over a year, what have your gains been?"

"I have my lodging free."

"And?"

"I have had nine shillings to buy a petticoat, two silver bodkins and the £2 of which I told you."

"What is the sum total of Swift Nick's transactions?"

"I only know of the £2,000 he has from the road this year, and that is the most he has ever had. There are some carriers and mail coach drivers who pay him not to rob them, but I do not know how much."

"Such a menace to the district must be removed," said the man at the table. "Elizabeth Burton, since you have freely given information, I am inclined to clemency. Your wearing of men's garments is an offence for which, in the circumstances, I cannot punish you since a public whipping would alert Nevinson to the danger of his position. You will be given decent clothing and must leave the town immediately. If you ever return, you will be whipped and charged with the theft, and could well hang therefore."

It would go even worse with me if any of Nick's gang were aware of this morning's work. Homeless, penniless, encumbered by skirts and without my horse, I set off to walk the great North Road where I had so often ridden by moonlight. Nick was going to be caught and brought to justice. Since he came from Yorkshire, he was likely to be tried at York, and I intended to be there.

On the way I stopped at farms, begged or worked for food and lodging, and enjoyed being out of doors, free and solitary. By the time I reached York, I felt neither guilt, anger, nor fear, but only curiosity as to what the outcome of the trial would be.

When Nick was transported to Tangier it was a relief, for I did not want blood on my hands. Within five years he escaped and returned to this country and his old ways. For three years I remained afraid of his vengeance, until he was recaptured and sentenced to death.

They said he made a good end, asking forgiveness on the scaffold and warning others against a life on the road. Then he pulled the cap over his eyes and gave the hangman the signal that he was ready.

Perhaps he remembered the song about himself,

> *Did you ever hear tell of that hero*
> *Bold Nevinson that was his name;*
> *He rode about like a bold hero,*
> *And with that he gained great fame.*
>
> *He maintained himself like a gentleman*
> *Besides he was good to the poor;*
> *He rode about like a bold hero,*
> *And he gained himself favours therefore.*

37

Ringing for Gopher

A man thinks best alone and out of doors. I take my pipe, put on a stout pair of shoes and make for the River Trent whenever I wish to ponder on my affairs.

These wide flat spaces are soothing; a little melancholy, perhaps, but the sunsets over the River Trent are spectacular at this time of year, and of course the watery landscape reminds me of my home in the Netherlands.

I have need to return there on occasion, for the Bank of Amsterdam finances a good part of Europe, being far in advance of any English bank; but for the rest, this town of Newark serves me very well. I like the sound sense of its citizens, they are solid and considerate; the pace of life is comfortable to a man of my age and inclinations.

The town is well-built, trade is good, and with my knowledge of drainage I hope to make Newark an even more prosperous place by creating more fertile land in the marshes of the River Trent. Therefore I have the best of reasons to take my solitude in an area I love.

So many floods make for a rich loam; fat crops will grow here when the excess of water is controlled by deep dykes and sluices. There will be good pasture too for cattle with a mixture of herbs and grasses that will give excellent flavour to butter and cheese, as well as this famous English roast beef which I enjoy.

Such satisfying thoughts naturally draw my eyes skywards where the amethyst and rose shades of evening recall the splendour of beautiful fabrics, the merchanting of which is my other love. In fact my father still runs our family house, dealing in silks and velvets and supplying me a small amount for select customers. The burghers of Newark have a fondness for display.

As the light fades this November afternoon, a trail of mist rises above the rank tussocks which thrive on moisture, and the air becomes chill. Climbing a bank and gazing over the landscape, I am apprehensive to notice that not too far away the mist is knee high and advancing towards me like a ghostly tide. Above me rides a slender new moon, and I resolve to make all speed home.

But as I press on the vapour rises and thickens until I am drowned in cold blindness and utterly confused. One step more and I slip from the bank to be immersed in standing water that reaches above my knees. I clutch at rushes and stagger out with mud filling my shoes, my feet and legs benumbed. Would I could move quickly enough to revive the circulation, but all sense of direction is lost and I cannot see the pitfalls that lie at my feet.

A shape looms out of the fog, a bent and crooked thorn that resembles an old man and I lean against its rugged trunk trying to peer through the cloud, to listen for the cough of human or animal that might guide me to a habitation. My ears ache and my eyes burn with strain. I am desolate indeed.

By way of lessening my loneliness I speak aloud, warning myself against the danger of falling into the river and so perishing. The words that come to me are those of a psalm which I had often thought comforting, and never have I needed comfort as I do now.

> *My help cometh even from the Lord who hath made heaven and earth.*
> *He will not suffer thy foot to be moved: and he that keepeth thee will not sleep.*
>
> *The Lord shall preserve thee from all evil;*
> *Yea it is even he that shall keep thy soul.*
> *The Lord shall preserve thy going out and thy coming in,*
> *From this time forth for ever more.*

There is power in the words, enough to make me stand up and cast around. Now I bethink me, St Paul says *We walk by faith, not by sight*, and so I will. If only I could hear, and so guide myself as do the blind.

*They that wait upon the Lord shall renew
their strength; they shall mount up with wings
as eagles; they shall run and not be weary;
they shall walk, and not faint.*

What a magnificent church it is, that one of Mary
Magdalene in the market place at Newark. I swear I can
see its tall spire rising out of the fog.

Listen. Listen, there are the very bells, sounding out
across these wastes. If I walk toward the sound and
beware the Trent, I shall be guided to safety.

Gopher, you have been a fortunate man this night. The
bells ring clearer, tread carefully now. When you reach
home, be sure to thank God for your deliverance. More
than that, give money for the ringers, and establish it for-
ever that at this season the bells shall ring out to guide
those who may be lost, as I have been.

*The Drovers'
Road*

The Rebel Stone

I knew Lachie was not to be trusted the way he came creeping round my mother just after Father died. Worse still, he started hinting I ought to be earning my own bread, being a well-grown lad of twelve, instead of hanging after the Dominie and thinking of going to college where I would likely learn nothing of use in the world.

"Nae doot wanting to wear a clean shirt to work, aye?" he asked.

I thought a clean shirt would suit me fine, but said nothing, and my mother told me sharply not to sulk. Lachie had brought her a good piece of scarlet wool from Lincoln to make a kirtle, and while she was pleased with the gift was worried the neighbours might think her over anxious to put aside her black.

She was also concerned about other matters. So soon after the rising of the '45 there were Jacobite sympathisers throughout Scotland, and English agents hunting them. My father had been for Prince Charlie, though he had not taken arms. All the same there were long memories where siller was on offer for information.

Lachie had words with Jock the Drover who took cattle south to the English markets. I was to go with him and his men, learning the job, making myself useful any way I could, though Jock boasted that the dogs, Flint and Jess, did the work and all we had to do was follow them and the herd.

My mother packed me a bag of meal, some onions, and a spare coat and breeks. Lachie gave me a knife, telling me it was a skene-dhu for my stocking. While Jock's men did not look like blackguards, I thought it a comfort to have by me at nights, though whether I would be able to use it in case of need was another matter.

There were two hundred head of small black beasts, sleek and well-fleshed, though I fancied they might be leaner by the time they reached the butcher. We set out at first light in early frost that brought a few leaves fluttering down. I shivered and felt the pull of my bed in the corner of the bothy, knowing I would not see it for many a long week.

Walking all day at the slow pace suited to the animals was unexpectedly tiring. By midday my head was jarring with every step, and my shoulders carried an invisible sore burden. Thereafter all pains joined and I was one lump of misery until we came to our first night stop.

When I would have sat dangling my swollen feet in the burn, Jock sharply sent me to gather wood, while Red Euan set about gutting a rabbit he'd caught with his sling, and the brothers Rab and Davey slipped among the hedgerows seeking herbs and roots for the pot. The cattle continued browsing while the light lasted, but we had not hurried and they had eaten their fill on the way. As the sun sank, they settled themselves to rest, and I built up a good fire to warm us and cook our food.

Fed and rested, I gazed up at the sky, noticing for the first time in my life the wondrous pattern of stars against the deep blue.

"How d'ye like the look of the sky?" asked Red Euan.

"Fine," I said, "The rabbit you caught was good."

"There's still the taste of corn in the flesh at this time of year," he said. "Later they get stringy, and when the fat's gone, so has the flavour."

"What about the beasts?" I asked, "Won't they find less to eat when the pasture is frosted?"

"We're travelling south, remember," he said. "Winter follows us. There's more than a month's difference in season between here and Doncaster."

"And dinna forget," said Jock, who had walked up to us, "that there are fields hired between here and London where they'll bide a day or two tae catch their wind. Now Lad," he went on, "Yon Lachie says you can read."

"Aye, I can."

He had taken out of his leather pouch an important

looking piece of vellum with a heading in fancy script which I was soon to recognise as a droving licence. All legal documents had this elaborate penmanship, and the words they used were similarly ornamental, but I managed to make out that Jock was permitted to convey cattle along recognised ways between Scotland and London at a price agreed with the owners, paying all charges for fodder and grazing, highway tolls and wages for hired hands. He was also allowed to carry a gun, sword, and pistol to protect the herd from reivers. It was signed by three magistrates.

I knew that Jock showed it to humble me for thinking droving lowly work. He then showed me letters that he had to deliver in the towns we passed through. They had been entrusted to him by those who knew him respectable and worthy, despite his rough appearance.

When I looked taken down, Jock struck out even keener. "Hae ye anything about you?" he asked, "Anything you're taking for Lachie?"

"What would I have?" I asked, but I knew what he meant. Lachie travelled the drovers' roads as often as any; he had money, but no work; and when he was away, as often as not, those who had fought for the Cause disappeared. Sometimes they hid in the hills for a week or two. Other times they took the road south in chains.

Jock said no more, but looked hard at me for a long moment, then grunted and turned away. I knew then there was much to be learned outside of any college.

Euan put his arm across my shoulders. "C'mon then," he said, "let's see you settled for the night in a guid dry bed without draughts."

He drew me away from the valley, pointing out the sparseness of turf where the wind scoured, and showed me a hollow sheltered by a low-growing thorn with leaves still green. "As warm a spot as you'll find," he said, and true enough I slept easily beneath the wide sky.

Day followed day. There were alarms when thieves threatened, but Jock and his men were formidable guards. We heard of other herds stricken by cattle plague, and twice had to take a detour where roads had been closed because of it. We took several rest days then, and bled the cattle as a precaution. Afterwards we mixed the blood with our oatmeal and onions for extra nourishment. By then we were in lands where it would have been dangerous to take a rabbit, for southern squires regarded all wildlife as their game.

The laird hereabouts, the Duke of Newcastle, had a very fine mansion and great park.

"Aye, well, is he not some bigwig in the English government?" asked Euan.

"Indeed, and stowing poor laddies in rotten ships at Tilbury to wait for trial," said Jock.

We passed under great trees and pressed on to the town of Tuxford where we would spend the last night of our journey before reaching Newark-on-Trent, the market there being our goal. Although Jock would travel on to London and beyond, this was a small herd, it would not pay to take them further than we need. Newark was a prosperous market. They would sell there well enough.

Tuxford was a bonny town winding uphill, with a good inn, the Red Lion and a meal waiting. We took the cattle out onto the southern edge where there was an enclosure. As we walked back, I noticed a great stone at the roadside with this inscription:

Here Lyeth

A   b

1746

The gap between words and date interested me. I thought I could make out some letters, perhaps 'A' followed by the space of three, then 'b'. Euan seemed anxious only for his food and edged away. I remembered that he had little schooling, perhaps could not read, and followed him to the

The Rebel Stone

inn.

Next day we set off joyfully, especially Jock who was looking forward to his profit, but we would all get our dues, even me.

As we reached the stone, I asked Jock what it was.

"Can you not see it's a gravestone?" he asked.

"It says 'Here Lyeth,'" I said, "but who?"

"Look at the date," he said, "and use your heid."

He strode away, leaving me smarting at what I took as a rebuke, knowing that 1746 was a year when many Scots had been taken to London for trial after supporting Bonnie Prince Charlie, but I was young and curious as to the identity of one who had been given a stone to mark his resting place.

Two guineas was my share of the £500 Jock drew, but he had expenses on the journey in tolls and pasturage, as well as the wages of Rab and Davey. They were minded to buy small goods to peddle at farms on the way back. Euan and Jock still had business to attend to and would likely find a ride home. My face must have shown that I was unsure of the way.

Jock laughed. "Flint and Jess will look after you as well as they do the stirks," he said.

"You'll no have to dawdle," grinned Euan, "they'll be back on the braes inside a week."

I could not believe the dogs remembered the slow miles we had trekked since starting all those weeks ago, but when we reached the Red Lion late that evening, it was clear the landlord was expecting us all. For them he had scraps and bones, for me a good broth and a bed in the byre.

He seemed kind, and I was already missing Jock and the others.

"Can you tell me who is buried under the big stone at the parish edge?" I asked.

"A rebel," he replied.

So that was how the letters fitted. I remembered the A–b pattern.

"What was his name?" I asked, still smarting at the word "rebel."

"Some say Lord Kilmarnock."

It could not be. Lord Kilmarnock had been tried and executed at Tower Hill.

"Must've been important," the landlord was saying, "to have a stone like that."

"No compliments in the epitaph," I said, "but the accusation is almost worn away already."

"Thanks to your droving fraternity," he grinned, "rubbing and scouring whenever they passed. Small blame to 'em; the man hadn't been tried after all."

From what I'd heard a trial would have made no difference, since the English government could find all the evidence they wanted against any brought out of Scotland. And if Prince Charlie had won there'd have been some ready to act the same toward those who had fought against him.

The next morning was cold indeed. Flint and Jess were ready to be off in the grainy early light, wolfing their food and rushing out, only to come back urging me to follow. I soon stumbled after and we made good speed to Bawtry where food again awaited us, to be paid for by Jock next time he passed. I pondered often on the trust between working folk when their rulers were aye suspicious.

Better by far for the unknown Scot to have died on the journey, and ended his suffering at the hands of those who would have his life by falsehood if they could not get it any other way.

Retracing that first journey in my mind, I wished him peace.

Fortune Telling

"Bennett! Bennett! Up you get! Take a warming pan to Mr Arthur's room at once. Turn down his bed properly, the way Timson showed you. He's come home late and is chilled."

The housekeeper was gone in a rustle of skirts, and I shook my head to clear it from the fuzziness of sleep. I was twelve years old, and this was my first place. At five this morning, I had scrubbed the front steps of the house on Northgate where my employers lived. After that I had helped various other servants, learning to make myself useful everywhere in the house, finally being given the job of freshening the carpet by putting used tea-leaves on to it and brushing them off with a hand-brush. It was a large carpet. I had amused myself by imagining the scroll pattern was a road-map, picturing the scenery along each road as I brushed, making up a story which happened along the way. Mrs Wheatley, the housekeeper, said I had done a very good job.

I was sorry about that, because I knew that after these first days they would decide what my abilities were and give me a position which would make best use of them. I did not want to be scrubbing floors for the rest of my life.

Now I had to — what had Mrs Wheatley said? Turn down the bed in Mr Arthur's room? I was confused. What time was it?

Still struggling with the buttons of my uniform because my fingers were cold, I made my way down the flagged passage to the servants' hall where the warming pans hung. Squinting at the big kitchen clock while raking hot embers into the copper pan, I saw that it was only eleven-o'clock. It had seemed like the small hours.

Tomorrow was Newark May Fair and my half day off. I was going with my friend Betty, determined to enjoy every minute, resenting lost sleep that would make me sluggish and dull.

"What are you up to?" asked Betty when I scurried into our bedroom on the top floor, still holding the warming pan. "You'll be skelped!" she said as I dragged it across the sheets on my bed and quickly dropped the blanket over to keep in the heat.

"Hop out for a minute and I'll do yours," I said, "It's so cold tonight it must be a late frost."

She rolled over and left a space in the middle which I warmed, then snuggled down gratefully as I rushed downstairs to return the pan. We would both sleep better in the warm nests I had made.

Next morning the thought of our outing helped us through the usual jobs, and after washing up the dinner dishes from the kitchen we were allowed to set off.

My intention was to go to the play booth, for I loved anything to do with acting and filled my head with imaginary dramas. Admission would cost fourpence, and Betty thought this too much. She wanted to have her fortune told.

Before the performance we could see the free parade of the actors and acrobats in fantastic costumes. I was longing to see "Maria Martin and the Murder in the Red Barn," and ignored the mingled smells of new corduroy, mothballs and beer which filled the tent.

At first we found the loud, exaggerated tones of the actors distracting, but as the audience settled down we found we were following the story as keenly as anybody there. There were gasps as Maria approached the barn to meet her death. We came out feeling shaken and weak.

We bought gingerbread, watched the boys at the coconut shies and hung around the fortune tellers, which we could not afford. "Your Destiny for a Shilling," proclaimed one placard.

A boy was standing near, looking as if he would like to enter the fortune teller's tent, but his friends were standing nearby, obviously watching to see what he would do and finding his dilemma amusing. To cover his embarrassment, he turned and spoke to us. "Did you enjoy the play?" he asked, "I saw you in the tent."

"It wasn't that good," said Betty, "but I liked it in a way."

The other boys came over. They were wearing Magnus Grammar School ties and caps, and were older than us, probably about sixteen.

"D'you know Tom Foy?" asked one.

It was a funny name, and I looked puzzled. "Donald here," he said, "it's a part he plays. He's quite a well known actor."

Donald, or Tom Foy, was quite red in the face, but spoke carefully and politely. "I wouldn't say that but I would like to be an actor. Only I don't see how I can manage it. My parents want me to take an exam to go in the Navy."

"I thought Miss Garner wrote the idiot's part for you," said one of the boys.

The idiot's part? I looked at Donald. His face was unusual, not really boyish, heavy and older. As I looked, he changed and gave a sly, half-witted sort of smile that at once chilled and amazed.

The boys applauded and asked for more. Donald had resumed his normal expression.

"You see," said the boy who had last spoken, "he really can act. You are going to be in the pantomime at Averham, aren't you Wolfit?"

"I'll have to ask my father," he said and moved away.

I watched him go, knowing that he was different from the other boys, knowing also his acting would be very different from that we had watched this afternoon. I would love to see the pantomime, and realised that whatever he had said about his father not allowing it, somehow one day he would be an actor.

As it became dusk and the lights came on, the shabbiness gave an air of romance to the cobbled square, watched over by the slender spire of the parish church. Tingling with the excitement of it, we made our way back to the big house in Northgate quite satisfied with the afternoon's entertainment.

Next morning Mrs Wheatley set me to do some sewing, which pleased me because my mother was a good needle-woman. She had taught me in the hope that, in time, I would become a nursery maid and gradually rise to become almost the equivalent of a lady's maid, so far as such persons were recognised in Newark. Even well-to-do tradesmen's wives preferred their "girls" as they called them to be general domestics and not give themselves airs.

In this case, it was mending some curtains which had become worn and frayed. The flower pattern was delicate and colourful and I selected the shades that matched, working the patch in almost invisibly.

"How beautifully you've done that," said a pretty voice that was certainly not Mrs Wheatley's, and I turned round to see one of the young ladies of the house. "I wanted to use those for my costume, the pattern is so right for the underskirt, it will look exactly like embroidery. Thank you very much."

"Yes, and you can have that sea-green bedspread for the bodice and overskirt," said her mother's voice and I scrambled to my feet dropping wools, needle, and scissors on the floor.

The mistress of the house laughed. She was not nearly as frightening as her housekeeper, and the girl helped me to pick up my things.

"Go and get the illustration you were given, Mary," she said to her daughter, "and you can take it round to Mrs Bennett with Lucy now. She'll get your measurements and make a start."

My father probably had bread and cheese for his dinner that day. Mother abandoned all her household work in order to make an immediate start on the costume required by Miss Mary for the pantomime in which she had a small part.

At first, I visualised a tent like the one we had visited at the May Fair, but it seems that a Vicar, called the Reverend Cyril Walker of Averham village, had built a theatre in his garden. He had found a lady called Miss

Kitty Garner to write plays for him when he did not write his own, and a number of children and adults to act in them.

Better still, the wife of the director of the town's important ball-bearing factory, had been a popular member of the D'Oyley Carte Company, and she helped to direct the plays. Her name had been Jessie Bond, which I thought very pretty, but now of course she was Mrs Lewis Ransome.

Miss Mary told me all this in breathless excitement while we walked back. She would be travelling to rehearsals in a wagonette that set off each evening from the Saracen's Head in the market place. The dates of the performance were set for a time of full moon to make travelling easier for both actors and audience.

Suddenly I was involved in activities unknown to me a few weeks before. Betty also became interested in strangers calling at the house and the groups of young people gathering in the old nursery, practising lines, trying on costumes and learning to use stage make-up. The whole household came to life in a most unexpected way.

There was trouble about Miss Mary travelling in the wagonette, chiefly because it was not considered suitable for her to walk to and from the Saracen's Head by herself after dark.

"Of course she will not walk alone," her mother said, "Lucy Bennett is a sensible girl, she can travel with her and help with her costume. When they return, I am sure Lucy's father will meet them both. I shall speak to him."

So it was that I went to that wooden theatre in the vicarage garden and helped Miss Mary dress. I still love to remember the excitement of the journey in the wagonette through the lamplit streets and out into the moonlit country lanes.

When the performance began, I crept into the wings and watched Donald Wolfit play the part of So-so, the Princess's suitor. But to my amazement, he had also learned the part of Abanazar the Magician and occasion-

55

ally played it. I listened to the applause of the audience and thrilled to his success. It was all so much better than the play booth at the May Fair, yet I knew seeing the one had helped me to appreciate the other, and that clever as Donald was even then, he had much in common with the barnstormers he had watched as eagerly as Betty and I.

The Great War was in its fourth weary year. Each week more young men disappeared from Newark for France. We spent our spare time knitting gloves and mittens for the troops, were allowed to help at concert parties to entertain the wounded, and saw Donald shine there in comedy roles.

There was a special feeling of belonging, of working together to produce the best that we could and of being valued for what we could do.

Donald Wolfit went on to become a world famous actor, while I continued scrubbing floors, meanwhile snatching at every chance to get as much out of life as I could.

After the war it became easier. Less places for domestic servants meant women doing what had once been considered men's work, and factories were prepared to offer us employment — at lower wages, of course.

Not only that, but bigger shops like Marks and Spencer came to Newark and wanted young lady assistants. Opportunity arrived.

Two great opportunities had already come my way. The first was learning the discipline of a well-run home; the second discovering leisure is more than time spent resting after work.

It sounds simple, but then having had no schooling since I was twelve, I'm a simple person. All the same, I've been happy in my way, finding interest in everything I do and in people I meet.

I wonder whether girls today are better off than we were. I suppose it depends what you make of yourself.

FURTHER READING

Bonser, Kenneth John
The Drovers : Who they were and how they went
(Macmillan) 1970

Brown, Cornelius
History of Newark
(Whiles, Stodman St, Newark) 1904

Roberts, David E.
The Battle of Stoke Field
(Newark and Sherwood District Council) 1987

Samuels, John
History Around Us
(Cromwell Press)

Smith, Stan
Nan Scott, The Face at the Window
(J.H. Hall and Sons Ltd) 1993

NOTTINGHAMSHIRE WRITERS
PUBLISHED BY FIVE LEAVES

David Belbin — *Dead Guilty*
156 pages, 0 907123 58 9, £4.99
(Young adult fiction)

David Belbin — *Haunting Time*
195 pages, 0 907123 62 7, £4.99
(Young adult fiction, short stories)

David Belbin (ed) — *City of Crime*
Crime fiction by Catherine Arnold, Robert Cordell, Michael
Eaton, Raymond Flynn, John Harvey, HRF Keating, Robert
McMinn, Stanley Middleton, Peter Mortimer, Brendan
Murphy, Julie Myerson, Frank Palmer, Alan Sillitoe and
Keith Wright
248 pages, 0 907123 12 0, £7.99

David Belbin & John Lucas (ed) — *Stanley Middleton
at Eighty*
178 pages, 0 907123 38 4, £9.99
(Essays)

Michael Billig — *Rock'n'Roll Jews*
168 pages, 0 907123 53 8, £7.99
(Music)

Judy Cox — *Robin Hood: Rebel and Outlaw*
12 A6 pages, 0 907123 11 2, £0.35

David Crouch and Colin Ward — *The Allotment:
Its Landscape and Culture*
320 pages, 0 907123 91 0, £12.99

Robert Gent (ed) — *Poems for the Beekeeper:
An Anthology of Modern Poetry*
138 pages, 0 907123 82 1, £6.99

John Lucas — *The Radical Twenties: Writing, Politics and Culture*
263 pages, 0 907123 171, £11.99

Pauline Lucas — *Evelyn Gibbs: Artist and Traveller*
108 pages, 0 907123 83 X, £9.99
(Biography)

Stanley Middleton — *Holiday*
240 pages, 0 907123 43 0, £7.99
(Fiction, winner of the Booker Prize)

Malcolm Seymour — *Mansfield Tales*
46 pages, 0 907123 13 9, £3.99
(Short stories)

Alan Simpson MP — *Beyond the Famished Road: New Policies for Common Security*
32 pages, 0 907123 27 9, £2.50

Keith Taylor — *Favourite Walks in Three Counties: Nottinghamshire, Derbyshire and Leicestershire*
156 pages, 0 907123 28 7, £6.99

Sue Thomas — *Water*
162 pages, 0 907123 51 1, £7.99
(Fiction)

Gregory Woods — *This Is No Book: a Gay Reader*
112 pages, 0 907123 26 0, £6.95

Five Leaves' titles are available from bookshops or, post free, from Five Leaves, PO Box 81, Nottingham NG5 4ER